Walter Crane, Euphemia J. Richmond

In the Fire

And other Fancies

Walter Crane, Euphemia J. Richmond

In the Fire
And other Fancies

ISBN/EAN: 9783337252670

Printed in Europe, USA, Canada, Australia, Japan

Cover: Foto ©Andreas Hilbeck / pixelio.de

More available books at **www.hansebooks.com**

IN THE FIRE.

·IN·THE·FIRE: BY·EFFIE·JOHNSON·

·LONDON: ELKIN·MATHEWS·VIGO·ST·
·1892·

IN THE FIRE

AND OTHER FANCIES

BY

EFFIE JOHNSON

WITH A FRONTISPIECE BY WALTER CRANE

LONDON
ELKIN MATHEWS
AT THE SIGN OF THE BODLEY HEAD
IN VIGO STREET
1892

LONDON :
PRINTED BY WERTHEIMER, LEA AND Co.
CIRCUS PLACE, LONDON WALL, E.C.

To the Friends whose sympathy has been
to me the source of many grateful memories,
I affectionately dedicate this Book.

2, VILLAS-ON-THE-HEATH,
         HAMPSTEAD,
    November, 1891.

CONTENTS.

IN THE FIRE.

T was Christmas-time, and the soft snow not only lay upon roof, hillside, hedge and tree, but it was falling. Gently and softly it was falling from the leaden sky above to the white earth beneath; and in its fall it seemed to level all the small inequalities of earth —as does the purifying influence of heaven-sent sorrow.

But inside the parlour all was warmth and brightness, for there was a splendid, old-fashioned fireplace in it, piled high to-night, with coal and logs ablaze, which gave out a glorious heat. Before the fire, upon the hearthrug lay little Rosie, fascinated by its flickerings.

" I can see the Fire King's grottoes. How beautiful they are! Oh, how I should like to walk about in them myself!" she exclaimed aloud.

And a very short time afterwards she seemed to be standing on the top bar of the large grate, as the Fire King took off his flaming cap to her in the friendliest manner possible.

"Come in, little girl, come in!" he called out, and a number of tiny flame-men, who danced in a train behind him, echoed heartily, "Come in." So in Rosie walked, all among the delightful grottoes of red-hot coal, and as something very, very wonderful seemed to have happened to her, she was not even scorched by the heat, but felt it to be pleasant and invigorating.

"Procession! Procession!" immediately commanded the Fire King to the tail of flame-men behind him. "Take our little girl guest round the kingdom!" and his voice sounded peremptory and crackly. Then he himself took Rosie by the hand and led her about the fire-kingdom.

She found it full of delightful surprises.

None of the chambers were at all alike.
Wander where they would, each glowing grotto
or cave-like chamber they entered was different
in shape and size from the one they left behind; and as there were no staircases, these led
one from another, up or down, in the most de-
lightfully higgledy-piggledy style imaginable.

Rosie found the variety more and more
interesting.

If you began to go anywhere there was
never any telling whether you would reach it
or some other place; and this, without trains to
catch or appointments to keep, was in itself an
entertainment!

But for the Fire King's hand, however,
Rosie would have been lost over and over
again. As it was, they went merrily on, all
the little flame-men dancing behind them.

"To the kingdom-top where the fire-breeze
plays!" shouted the King suddenly, and
twisting about, he promptly drew Rosie up-
wards to the top of the fire.

There the fire (which they here called the

" fire-breeze ") burnt uproariously of course ;
and they all scampered and romped about in it
famously, until the procession was merged
into a wild dance of promiscuous flame. Soon
Rosie herself caught the spirit of joy and
consuming haste which seemed to actuate
everyone else, and springing about with the
Fire King, her hair and dress began to move
about as quickly as the fire-breeze itself, which
enveloped and wrapt them all round with such
invigorating restlessness.

Altogether it was the most wonderful dance
anyone ever took part in, this dance of the
fire-breeze on the top of the fire, for it was a
dance of hard work and aspiration ; and that is
why it was so refreshing.

It warmed, not only the flames themselves
that took part in it, but all Rosie's family as
well, who sat at tea wondering why she slept so
long on the hearthrug, yet not liking to disturb
her ; and it cheered all who looked on.

Great lumps of black coal and dark boughs
of wood changed into glorious, glowing sub-

stance under its aspiring energy; and were
finally borne up the great chimney, dark as
pitch, to sail as films of smoke nearer the
tranquil stars.

Well might Rosie rejoice in it!

But suddenly all were crushed down!
Rosie's father was putting coal on.

What was the consequence of that?

Well, in a moment the Fire King had pulled
Rosie with him down to the stedfastly glowing
grottoes below, calling out, "Procession!
Procession! Escort our little girl guest to
the dining-hall, and leave the fire-breeze to
attack the fresh fuel."

So into form behind came the little flame-
men again, as the King gaily led Rosie back
to the very underneath part of the fire-kingdom, where a capacious, glowing chamber,
with irregularly buttressed, glowing walls, became their dining-hall.

"We don't like your family staring at us
while we have meals, so we generally dine out
of their sight, somewhere below and behind,"

said the King to Rosie; and his voice sounded
confidential and less crackly under the soothing influence of the dining-hall.

"I am sorry we have been rude," Rosie
rejoined with contrition; and indeed she was
sorry; she had never thought that she could
hurt any one's feelings by gazing into the fire.
"What do you eat?" she inquired, to turn the
conversation.

"Nice little bits of coal or wood," returned
the King; "you shall see how we do it."

Then he sat down at the end of a long,
glowing table, having placed Rosie at his
right hand; and the little flame-men sprang
from behind and sat down, too, along the sides
of it, while into the hall frolicked a procession
of fire cooks, all wearing flaming aprons, and
carrying glowing dishes in their hands, the
contents of which blazed up the moment
they entered the room. Doubtless these were
"nice little bits of coal or wood," as the
King had said.

Advancing towards the table, the chief cook

then put his dish right upon His Majesty's head, instead of placing it before him in a civilised manner, and then the rest of the cooks treated the rest of the flame-men in exactly the same way. Each put a flaming dish upon a head with considerable dispatch.

Then all the party blazed away comfortably together.

"And now," said the King, turning to Rosie, "now that you have seen how we take our meals, what will you, yourself, take? The table was put here entirely for your convenience, because we, of course, never need such a thing."

"Thank you," said Rosie modestly, quite relieved at having no flaming dish put upon her own head; "a little bread-and-butter, please."

The King was so very polite that the moment he caught what fell from her lips he called out in the crackliest voice imaginable, "Bread-and-butter, at once, for the little girl guest."

Then up sprang three energetic flame-men, up through the grottoes, out on to the bars of the grate, and from there to the table in the middle of the room, where they managed to get a tiny morsel of bread-and-butter; and then they hurried back with it to the fire again.

But, alas! alas! from no fault of theirs, of course, but all owing to the climate, by the time they had carried that morsel of bread-and-butter to the presence of Rosie and the Fire King, it had turned into the most disagreeable black toast possible, with the butter frizzling away in a frenzied manner on the top.

"Is this what you like?" asked the King, innocently, for he knew nothing whatever about bread-and-butter.

"Thank you; this is—toast, but it will do very nicely," Rosie managed to say, but in so hesitating a manner that the King at once detected something was wrong.

"Toast!" he ejaculated; "then—nonsense! for that is not what you wanted!"

"*Bread-and-butter* for the little girl guest!"
he cracked and frizzled out furiously.

"Yes, your Majesty," said the three flame-
men in a fright; and off they set again—up
through the glowing grottoes, out by the bars
of the grate to the table in the room where the
family sat at tea; and again they seized upon
another bit of bread-and-butter, and retired
with it to their own dining-hall as before.

But, alas! alas! all owing to the climate
again, of course, when they reached the King
and Rosie this bit was also burnt to a cinder.

With half a glance the King saw it was just
like the last, which Rosie had called "toast";
so, ordering these flame-men to sit down, with a
good deal of wrath, he signed to three others
to go on the quest again. Then, as these were
no more successful than the others had been,
the King, being a sensible creature, was
obliged to confess that he had ordered an
impossibility, and that it was out of his power
to procure bread-and-butter for any guest in
his own kingdom, however polite he might be.

So he led little Rosie back to the bars of the grate, and, waving farewell to her in his wonderfully friendly way, bade her go and have just what she liked to eat with her own family at their table.

At which moment Rosie woke up, and went to tea.

And afterwards, when she thought her adventures over, and told her father of them, while they sat cosily together in his armchair, he said that it was really a very interesting and curious time, this which she had passed in the fire-kingdom, and that it plainly taught him a lesson; it taught him this—whenever by any chance you do get out of your element in this world, you cannot stay there very long, because it is so next to impossible to find your requisite nourishment there!

THE RIVER.

LL you could see was the water, dropping from one stone to another on
the mountain side in a tiny waterfall.
It was a spring, which there issued
forth to thread its way down towards the foot
of the mountain, thence to the valley beyond,
and out into the wide world.

But this small spring had been making just
this same small beginning for many, many
years without knowing the result of its work.
Men had lived, and grown old, and died, trees
even had grown up and rotted away, positively
nations had risen and fallen while the mountain rill, so small and unnoticeable, had been
springing up in this everlasting beginning.

At length one of the swallows that bathed
his beak in the rill talked to her in the sunshine.

"Fresh rill," he said, "thank you for your refreshing coolness. So deliciously you spring up from beneath the sod. From time immemorial, so our swallow legends tell us, you have faithfully afforded us this refreshment whenever we have chosen to rest and take it. Is there any way in which *I* can serve you?"

Then the rill told the swallow her great desire. It was, to find out if she had been of any use in the world by constantly bubbling up in this way for so many hundreds of years. "Oh! swallow," she concluded, "you who have wings to use, fly—fly and see what the other end of this my small beginning is like; and tell me, for sometimes I *long* to know."

Without a word in reply the swallow lifted his beak from the rill, and, with his sinuous wings, flew down the mountain side, through the valley, and out into the wide world; and ever he flew beside and along the river which had its source in the mountain rill he wished to serve.

It was at first, he saw, only the very smallest

river, here and there in the valley spanned
by planks of wood, and cattle grazing in the
meadows near its banks stooped to drink its
waters as they lowed to each other across
it. Gradually, however, it grew wider and
stronger, through the influx of other streams
which ran to join it, and then turned great
water-wheels.

The bridges that spanned it henceforth were
built of stone or iron, arched and picturesque;
the houses on each side were large, with
gardens that nestled comfortably down to the
water's edge.

And cheery boatmen shouted or sang as
they launched or moored their boats upon it.

In short, the swallow noticed how useful the
river was, and what wholesome pleasure it
brought to all in its course; in its cheerful
rush energy to turn a water-wheel, or freshen
the air; in its quiet moods—soothing to those
who rowed or drifted upon its surface; and to
the ducks and water-fowl living upon it, the
river's was a very beneficent existence indeed.

Ever and anon armies of gnats, or solitary dragon-flies, danced above or darted across it.

By and by though, as the swallow still flew on, even these characteristics changed; and the river became so large and so wide that towns as well as houses were situated on its banks; large ships as well as boats floated upon it; and then, as it neared the sea, that wonderful force, the tide, began to move it.

Thus the other end of the tiny mountain rill was the mouth of a great river, moved by the same force that moves the ocean; and the swallow had learnt how mighty and powerful may be the end of a very small beginning.

But he had meanwhile learnt even more of the river's worth than his bird's-eye view could teach him; for as his sinuous wings allowed him to fly, or dart, or stop, in fact, do just as he liked, he had flown and darted about, and questioned many a thing upon the way.

"What good does the stream do?" he asked, first of all, of the blue forget-me-nots.

"But for the stream we could scarcely exist. We live in and love the streamlet," was their reply. He next put the question to the water-wheel, as it turned so busily round with a merry splash.

"Large as I am," he thundered in answer, "I could do nothing without the river! It turns me round, I set the machinery going, and that grinds the corn. I look upon the river as a very great power in the world: it certainly moves me more than anything else! Owing to the river I keep the mill going, and the flour we make together—that keeps the people going!" and the water-wheel turned round and round in such a fury of glad work that anything else he said was drowned in his own roar.

Then it occurred to the swallow to question the breeze as to what use the river was in the world.

"Ah!" she replied, "the river and I are very good friends. I follow her through the valleys, for she makes the way smooth for me.

Both the clouds and I are continually helped by the river."

The water-rats, too, bore their testimony to the river's usefulness. "What the country would do without it I cannot tell," said a large, wise, old one. "I have spent the best of my life in running about these banks, wearing out my teeth in eating up the rubbish I find; but the river does more than ever I can, for he just sweeps it away to the great hungry ocean! And after that," he continued, "even we water-rats need not trouble any more about it. To clear away refuse is a great work," he concluded with a heavy sigh; then he whisked up his long tail, and scampered to work again.

And, lastly, what news the seagulls told the swallow about the river, as they perched together in a ship's rigging at the river's mouth.

"Owing to the river these ships are enabled to carry their cargoes of sugar, and rice and coffee, that are in reality so much food and clothing for human beings; and all owing to this, too, towns spring up, and peoples flourish," said the seagulls, chattering all at the same time.

They knew these things so well, and were quite glad to be able to give a little information and have a talk with any one on the rigging.

So then the swallow returned to the very beginning of the river—the rill.

The sun was setting as he neared the mountain side again, so that it stood out like a purple mystery in the golden light of the sky behind it; but the swallow was able to find the rill, and when he reached her she was springing up as faithfully and cheerily as she had done for many hundreds of years, from sunrise to dew-fall, all the years through.

The swallow rested upon the stone, and after dipping his bill into her cool water, said, " Greeting and cheer I bring you, gentle rill, and news from the other end of you; thanks to my strong wings, I have been

able to fulfil your wish.   For many, many long
miles I have flown along the river which has
its rise in you."

And then the swallow gave the rill a faithful
account of all he had heard and seen ; and
convinced her that she was the source of im-
measurable good and use in this fair world.

So, thankfully the rill bubbled up from between the sods and the stones after that, and
merrily she danced down in a waterfall—more
merrily than ever, as the evening star beamed
over her for the hundred thousandth time.

"Henceforth," she whispered, "I shall be
content to contribute my humble beginning
to the river for ever and ever, now that I
know I am of some use in the world.   I will
never get disheartened again."

And the swallow who had cheered the
gentle rill pirouetted above and about her
in the gathering twilight for a while, then,
darting along the hillside, he dived through
the purple mystery into the golden light which
he loved.

MIRABEL.

 "I HAVE had enough, too much of love," said the stern King, in the midst of his grief; "take her away to my round tower on the cliff."

His beautiful wife had just died: he was nearly broken-hearted, and this he said of his infant daughter. He banished her soon after she was born lest he should grow fond of and have to lose her too.

The Court, as well, mourned the loss of their good Queen; but as the old Nurse Griseld and Maid Agnes bore the babe away, one of the ladies said: "It is the sweetest babe that ever was born; it will be lonely in the round Tower, so far away from us all!"

Three hundred stone steps, as steep as the cliff itself, led to the Tower.

"When she is old enough," said the stern King; "the man who can climb those steps shall have her, but with my consent she shall never come down from the Tower before that time," and he smiled a strange smile as he added—"and the man who ascends those steps will be worthy of her. She will be sure to like him."

And in spite of his grief he smiled again for a moment, a bright smile, as he thought of the future.

The people of the Court thought it sounded all very easy, and that any princess would soon be settled in life, if that was all a man had to do to win her; and they whispered among themselves that His Majesty might have chosen a severer test of a husband than that one; but then the people of that Court had never tried to mount those steps themselves, they had only looked at them in the distance.

So Dame Griseld and Maid Agnes, escorted by a body-guard, took the infant Princess to the Tower.

There was little difficulty for either of them in ascending the stone steps, they soon found this out when they began to do so; and they gazed up with interest at the round Tower, which stood at the top of the cliff, overlooking the plain below; but the King's body-guard fell and floundered, and floundered and fell, when they began to go up the steps, until at last every man of them gave up the attempt in despair.

Not one of them could do it. Each step seemed more difficult than the last; because an invisible weight seemed to drag them back as they ascended; so the body-guard settled at the bottom to watch, while the maid bounded up like a roe, and the old dame, who carried her precious charge, mounted in more stately fashion.

On either hand were dark woods. Who could tell what forms haunted these?

The body-guard below wound the cheery blast of a horn to comfort the dame and the girl; but this was not very much, when we consider they could have done nothing to help had any danger occurred. At last, Dame Griseld thinking so, turned round to dismiss them.

But the soldiers remained where they were, winding the horn at intervals, because they dared not return to the King until the Royal child was safely lodged in the Tower.

And this Tower, at the top of the steps, when at last the three who could, did reach it, what was it like?

Really beautiful! Neither very large nor very small, it was perfectly round, built of stone, dark with age, and almost covered with climbing creepers.

Narrow casement windows caught the sunlight, here and there, near the top or basement of the Tower; while the foliage of the creepers and their delicate flowers, lent grace to its rugged appearance.

Inside, when the maid and the dame entered, they found everything as fresh and dainty as is the heart of a flower; indeed, the very perfume of roses was in the air.

The archway by which they entered opened
by a short passage into a circular hall, the
centre of the Tower; and doors led from this
to different chambers on the ground-floor, a
staircase to the gallery above, whereon the
doors of the bedchambers opened.

A fountain played in the middle of the hall,
and upon its white marble basin were piled
fresh roses. Hence the perfume which filled
the Tower.

Dame Griseld took the infant Princess up-
stairs to the room prepared for her.

The colouring of this room and everything
in it was yellow—different tints and shades of
yellow, sweet and dainty.

The old nurse put the child into a crib to
sleep; then she took Maid Agnes over the
whole of the Tower.

One room contained dining-tables, and was
a deep damask in colouring; another, fitted up
with dark green lounges, pinked out here and
there with touches of faint blue.

The effect of every room was to induce

repose, while the atmosphere of each was redolent with the perfume of flowers, yet always
fresh.

Dame Griseld was quite satisfied with the
order in which she found everything; and in
truth she had reason to know when things
were as they should be, for she had lived
here before, many and many a year ago, when
the King himself was a child.

In these surroundings, then, the Princess
Mirabel grew up.

Her childhood, with its zest and quaintnesses,
and rushes of quick emotion, was gradually
left behind; her girlhood passed; and Mirabel
slept, and rose, and went about the Round
Tower, a graceful maiden, with her companions—Dame Griseld ever faithful, Maid
Agnes, young and gay.

Thus the Princess had experienced change
in herself during their seventeen years' resi-
dence in the Tower; but the two others did
not appear to have altered in the least.

"I know Dame Griseld is almost a hundred

years old," said Maid Agnes one day to the Princess, as they arranged the first roses of a new summer in the marble fountain basin.

"Who told you so?" inquired Mirabel.

"My grandmother," replied the girl. "She told me so when she heard that we were appointed by the King, your father, to attend you, lady, here. 'Dame Griseld is almost as old as the Tower itself is,' she said, so by that she must have meant very, very old."

"And how old are you, Agnes?" suddenly asked the Princess, pausing in her beautiful task to look her cheerful companion in the face.

"That I never can tell," replied the maid. "I am older than any one knows or thinks, yet I never look old, but always young, however much I grow up."

They both smiled and pursued their work.

Just then Dame Griseld, in snowy cap and large embroidered apron, came out of the damask room towards them.

She came and sat and watched them as they

arranged the flowers, for she loved her foster daughter and Maid Agnes well. And at this moment she said to herself, as she noticed a wistful expression on the young Princess's face, which of late she had seen there rather too often, " In spite of the peace and delights of this Tower, the child is lonely and needs other companionship."

And, though Dame Griseld said nothing aloud, she sighed and rose, then stooped and kissed the Princess where she sat, and left them.

Now the dame's thought was quite true. Mirabel was sometimes both sad and lonely in the Tower, she scarcely knew why. Many a time after she had completed her studies, finished her duties, and worked at her tapestry frame until she was tired, she would gaze down the great flight of steps, longing for—she knew not what; but it was evidently something the Tower did not contain. And sometimes, unknown to either of her companions, she would leave her dainty, yellow bed unpressed, and, wrapping herself up, go out by a staircase that led to the roof, and, in the moonlight, let her imagination range freely away, over the darkly-grouped trees that covered the cliff, to the mysterious plain beyond, where began, as it seemed to Mirabel, the wide, wide world. Frequently at these times she had wished for the wings of a bird, that she might fly where her imagination urged her; but then her father's decree would occur to her, and she would remember that a lover would one day come to lead her forth. She must wait.

But the time seemed long.

However, at last they had reached another early summer; and the morning after the first roses had been placed in the hall was fresh and fair as morning could be.

A frolicsome breeze waved the growing meadow-grass on the plain beneath, and was sporting in reckless mood with the sedate Tower itself, when its inmates were pleasurably disturbed at their early occupation by the winding sound of a horn.

At once Maid Agnes went to the window to see what this might portend.

And there, at the foot of the three hundred steps, were a dozen princes at halt on horseback. Again the horn sounded melodiously.

Dame Griseld's heart both bounded and sank, for *she* knew at once what this meant; and the Princess Mirabel, as she stepped through the archway to the top of the steps, followed by her two companions, blushed, for she too guessed that these were wooers who had at last come.

Maid Agnes replied to them on a silver horn.

When the cavalcade beneath heard the clear response and caught sight of the lovely princess standing there, her dark hair blown by the wind behind her, they broke into an enthusiastic greeting.

" We Princes are here," called out a voice from below, " all of us, with the King's consent, pledged to try and win the Princess's hand."

" Then which of you can climb the stone steps. Let us see!" replied Dame Griseld, taking the Princess Mirabel fondly by the arm. " The one who reaches the top the Princess will be sure to like," added the old dame to herself, remembering the King's words!

Whereupon began a bustle and stir among the Princes below, as to who should try his luck first.

At length they seemed to have settled the matter, for presently the eldest among them came forward to begin the ascent, while the others watched him. To judge from his demeanour this Prince was a proud man, of handsome build.

It seemed to the rest that the mere fact of his trying was the very doom of every other individual's chance. But, to the amazement of all, he had not gone more than six steps up the flight before he fell, and heavily too.

Nothing daunted, however, he rose and tried again and again, but it was of no use, his attempts all ended in failure; so at last, with a half-ashamed, though polite bow to the Princess, he gave up the ordeal, and, mounting his horse, rode away.

A shout of unrestrained gladness burst from his rivals as they saw him go; and Mirabel felt no disappointment.

Another Prince then came forward, another, and yet another followed him; indeed, each now became so impatient to try his luck, that they could wait in turn no longer, but began all together to take the ascent anyhow.

Few of them got far up, however; and those that did found the greatest difficulty in getting higher still; meanwhile the Princess regarded them all with interest and amusement rather than deeper emotion; while it must be confessed that Maid Agnes made merry in her own mind at their expense.

Yet, although the Princess had not until now noticed one among the many suitors who roused her liking, she watched them all with interest; for, be it remembered, she had never seen any of the opposite sex before.

At last, however, as she was leaning forward to mark which of the Princes were still struggling up, and which of them had left off in despair, she noticed for the first time that a fair young Prince—as fair as her own wishes —was leaving all the rest far behind; and as the Princess, thus looked down upon him he looked up at her and, meeting her glance with a quick, sweet smile, gracefully bared his head as he gazed at her in return.

And something sprang up between them there and then. It must have been love; for after that the Princess wished with her whole soul that he might reach her.

From that instant she scarcely saw the others—scarcely indeed noticed that one after another they were falling heavily, and giving up their efforts to ride away dejected; for her heart and gaze were alike ·concentrated upon this particular Prince.

And surely he felt it; for such strength came to him, such buoyancy, such hope and joy, that, flinging himself with renewed vigour

again to the attempt, he succeeded in getting
higher and higher up the flight of steps.

Meantime the morning had worn away; it
was noon, and the sun's heat poured down
upon the suitors—the few that remained—
making their ascent a hard toil; and always the
fair young Prince kept steadily ahead of them.

Yet sometimes he too fell beneath the invisible weight which was so soon to entirely
vanquish all the others; but upon finding that
the gentle Princess still watched him with un-
wearied interest, he would rise and struggle
on again.

And now the sun set; the glory of purple
and golden clouds lay against the faint tints
of a pure sky.

Then Dame Griseld came anxiously to her
charge, and tried to entice the Princess in to
their evening repast; but Mirabel would not
move.

Dame Griseld, therefore, went in alone.

Twilight came on; still Mirabel sat waiting
at the top of the steps, waiting for the valiant

Prince, who, with laborious effort, mounted steadily towards her.

At last there were only a few paces between them, he looked to speak to her; but at this moment the mysterious weight dragging the Prince back became so powerful, that he fainted beneath it.

"Agnes! Agnes! quick, run to his aid!" called the Princess, in distress.

And, quick as thought, Maid Agnes, taking water and food, went to the Prince's succour.

She bathed his temples, and restored his senses, and then gave him nourishment.

He took it and ate, as he did so thanking the maid in a kind voice.

The moon rose. The Prince looked again towards his beloved bride elect.

She was still there, the moonlight on her pure brow and graceful robing, and now that he was so near her, his heart almost sickened with delight. Again he returned to his task, while the maid joined her mistress.

" What is it that drags them all down when they try to ascend the steps," said the Princess as Maid Agnes came up, " I cannot understand it."

" Lady," replied the girl, " it is well that you did not ask me in the daylight, for then I could see nothing ; but now, as the moon rises, I think I do see something. It is dark, and shadowy, but huge and monstrous. It darts out from the wood and pounces upon and burdens him. Look! look! *look!* lady, do you not also see it?" and the girl pointed in horror towards the bending and slowly advancing Prince.

" Can any shadow be so heavy to him ; or is it a fiend? It clings to his shoulders, and whispers in his ear! Dear lady, look."

But the Princess saw nothing except the Prince; and though she started at the intelligence that fell from the maid's lips, her eyes did not leave the nearing form of her beloved. If anything, her love for him increased, as tears of pity rose from her heart.

The maid, however, having seen the monstrous shadow, or whatever else it was, ran into the Tower terrified.

The Princess was thus left alone as the Prince came close up to the topmost step.

Again he raised his eyes to hers, and again his face flashed out delight.

Pain and his invisible burden now left him, and for a moment he stood upright, free from all hindrances—victorious!

He smiled and bent low before Mirabel, and taking both her hands in his kissed them tenderly.

And after his hard stuggle and her long waiting time, now, as they stood together in the moonlight, it was rapture to them.

Well might they love each other! And so much did they love each other, even at this, their first meeting, that it was long before they turned from the spot where they first clasped hands, and entered the Tower.

When they did so, however, Dame Griseld stood in the round hall to greet them.

"Rest you by this fountain, Prince," she said, as they approached, and she beckoned to Maid Agnes, and drew them all together to sit on the marble edge of the fountain, among the roses.

Then she said, " I will now tell you what that invisible power is which has tortured the Prince, and puzzled the Princess so much this eventful day."

So Mirabel learnt at last that the King had entrusted her old nurse with the secret from the very first.

" In these woods at each side of the flight of steps," continued the dame, " lives a mighty and wise magician, who devotes his whole life to guarding what the King sends to this Tower; and none but the very young, or the very old, can escape this magician's power. Everyone else who would mount the three hundred steps to reach the Tower, has to over- come it. And this is no easy task, as the Prince, through dear experience, has himself felt and shown us this day. The reason he has had such difficulty in coming here is owing to the magician's power.

"The wood is full of his messengers, who haunt it; and they have haunted it ever since long before I brought the Princess, a babe, in my arms, from her father's Court.

"And the curious trait about these, the magician's messengers, is that *they are invisible*, only on the rarest occasions can any one see them. And their one task is to try and test the patience and perseverance of any one who wishes to reach the Tower. No spells can be brought to bear against the magician's; nothing can resist them except the continuing patience of a good heart.

"That is the one and only thing which can triumph over his strange, invisible forces.

"So when the Princes arrived at the bottom of the steps this morning, bright though the sunshine was, the woods teemed with the magician's unseen accomplices; and the moment the Princes began to mount the steps, believing that because they saw nothing to hinder them from reaching the Princess that nothing was there, out and upon them sprang and pounced the invisibles, and tried to drag them down with a clinging, clogging weight.

"And as you, fair Prince, were the only one among them both willing and able to rise and try again after *every* fall, you only have been able to vanquish the magician's messengers, and to prove yourself by the King's test, to be worthy of the hand of his daughter. *You* have won the Princess in marriage; you are worthy of her, and you need never fear the magician's power again, for through your own efforts you have now put yourself out of the reach of it for ever."

And the Princess smiled with such pleasure upon hearing this, that the Prince felt he might—he must—and he did—kiss her!

And Dame Griseld concluded, as her eye lingered fondly on the happy pair, "So you see how wise and kind both the King and the magician were, for they have saved the

Princess from all the impatient, reckless men who have dared to hope for her, and arranged that she should become the bride of the only one whom she could love, the very one who deserves to have her."

So the Princess left the Round Tower, and went out into the wide, wide world, the good young Prince's bride.

THE TRIAL.

HE clock constituted himself the Judge, naturally enough; his position required that he should do so.

He stood in the middle of the mantelpiece, looking down over the rest of the things in the room.

Then, as the others said, his opinion ought to be weighty, when he had that heavy pendulum inside him always at work.

A very wide-awake thing, too, is the clock; he never thinks of going to sleep; and that is a highly desirable quality in a judge! So the others quite approved of his nomination.

It was the middle of the night when the clock was thus promoted; and all the things in that room had been quarrelling dreadfully. Some took this side and some that; and the case was called " The Cheerfulness of the

Canary *versus* The Greater Cheerfulness of Other Things in the Room."

So the ornaments at each side of the clock swore they were the Jury.

Upon this the poker and tongs jumped up on end, and declared they were pleading barristers. It was difficult for either of them to look up to the clock—they were both so stiffnecked; but what of that, when they knew that, however long they talked, he would not go to sleep?

"What is the matter?" said the Judge, as he took upon himself to open the case informally. "What is it all about?"

Then up jumped the newspaper from the table, and, before any one could prevent him, rattled off this information in reply:

"There was a fight last night in the room of a harmless and respectable old lady, Miss Prisms, spinster. The table knocked the chairs, the chairs kicked the table, the hearthrug rolled up and half-smothered the footstool, the screen stood in front of everything it could, and was as rude as possible, and the piano twanged out of tune to insult the score; the shelves half killed the books by tossing them out upon the floor, the keys locked up the doors, and then jumped out of the keyholes; and all because of a most trivial incident.

"A bunch of flowers had been brought in that morning, and placed upon the table in a vase by Miss Prisms, spinster, in the most innocent manner possible. (It was not even supposed by the lamb at dinner that a gentleman had given them to her.) However, the moment Miss Prisms turned her back the flowers fell to complaining among themselves. They said that, for their part, they much objected to being in prison; that they regarded the vase and the room as such, and nothing else; and then they went on to remark that most of the other things near them seemed to be in prison, too, and how wonderfully cheerful the canary was—singing away in his prison, the cage. They didn't understand how he could be so cheerful behind those bars!

" Thereupon the speaking likenesses upon the wall got eloquently angry about this praise of the canary.

They persisted that nobody could look and be more cheerful than they themselves were, in spite of their prison-like frames. One of them wore a perpetual smile, which was tiresomely cheerful. Then the rest of the things spoke out, some for the cheerfulness of the canary, agreeing with the flowers, and some for the greater cheerfulness of other things in the room, till at last there ensued a free fight."

After giving off all this information, the newspaper fell flat again.

The Judge said, " Tick, tack! I see."

" I'm for the canary's cheerfulness, my lud! " exclaimed the poker, springing up on end.

" And I'm for the greater cheerfulness of other things in the room," said the tongs, as he, too, rose.

" Tack! " said the clock. " Let the poker begin."

Whereupon the poker rose and strained his neck to speak, so that the judge and gentlemen of the jury should hear every word.

He had no hands and arms to wave about, of course, so he put as much expression as possible into the feat of standing on end.

"My lud, ladies and gentlemen, no one who has seen the canary can have failed to remark what a delicate yellow he is, and how sweetly and clearly he sings. To begin with then, my lud, the canary is particularly remarkable for two most cheerful characteristics—the colour yellow, and the habit of singing. Nobody can deny this.

"Now from times far distant the habit of singing has been regarded as an outlet for mirth and good spirits; and for quite as long the yellow sun and sunshine have been regarded as emblems of cheerfulness. I believe, if the truth were known," continued the poker, "we steel things are going quite out of fashion, for no other reason than because that interloping brass generation which is rising to take our place is yellow, and therefore more cheerful-looking than we. In short, I declare that yellow is cheerful, and cheerfulness is yellow!

" The cheerfulness of singing, too, is universally acknowledged. Everyone knows that the inhabitants of this house go about singing whenever they feel particularly glad. Even the spinster lady herself has been heard to sing a little softly once, after a very precise old gentleman had been to call upon her (the card-tray here confirmed this fact in a whisper to the desk wherein the love-letters lay), and when she goes out the servants sing as loudly as possible—if they are in a good temper, that is. But whoever heard of any one singing off a *bad* temper I should like to know?

" No one, except such as assist at that unnatural, artificial place, the Opera. And I am sure, my lud, no one in this room has the bad taste to go there!" (It was vain for the opera-glasses upon the shelf to protest here, nobody heard, stifled as they were in their own

case.) " I therefore maintain, without fear of
contradiction," continued the poker, "that
the canary who sings so much and is so ex-
ceedingly yellow is the most cheerful prisoner
in the whole room."

Thereupon the poker returned to his
stretched out, recumbent position.

But just as most of the things in the room
were thinking over his words and beginning to
agree with him, up jumped the tongs.

He argued that singing was by no means a
sign of cheerfulness, and pointing to a bright
red plaque upon the wall, asked if anybody
present could deny the cheerful appearance of
that plaque? As nobody attempted to do so,
he pointed out that this red plaque, though in
his opinion one of the most cheerful objects in
the room, had never sung a note in its life;
moreover, he truthfully declared that it had
not a spot of yellow upon it. Then he said,
pointing to the fire, " There is another of the
most cheerful objects in the room (unfortu-
nately it is out now, but my remarks would

apply to it if it were in). In my humble
opinion the fire is a far more cheerful object
than the kettle, yet the kettle sings, while the
fire doesn't; the fire only roars in a modest
and primitive manner, and that very occasionally; and yet, I contend, the fire's roar is
just as cheerful as the kettle's singing."
And then he went on: "Through the open
window we hear a dismal sound at times; it is
borne to us by the breeze from across the
common, we consider it most melancholy.
And what, my lud, you ask may it be? My
answer is, it is nothing more or less than the
donkey *singing!*

"Human beings, too, sing hymns sometimes
in this very room; and I challenge anyone
to say that the greater number of them are
cheerful. They *are not*. Some few may be,
but the majority are *not*. I protest that most
of them are so melancholy as to draw tears
from a heart of steel—my own, for instance.
Many a time, my lud, has the housemaid
found me rusty in the morning, owing to the

tears that have broken out all over me during
the Sunday evening singing of the wrong sort
of hymns, perpetrated by the mistress and her
friends!'' And thus the tongs continued until
the judge was obliged to give him a hint to
stop.

He did so by becoming very striking indeed
himself—he struck twelve; and the consequence was that the attention of all turned
from the tongs to the clock, and the tongs
sank down in about as crushed a condition
as it is possible for a pair of steel tongs to
be reduced to. And every one was very
pleased; because the things in that room, like
many people in the world at large, cared more
about matters being brought to a conclusion
than about sifting truth.

Most people, whether they enjoy the beginning or the middle of anything or not, are
invariably pleased at the prospect of its
coming to an end.

Therefore there was great satisfaction among
the things in the room when the long speech

of the tongs was stopped by the clock striking twelve.

"After all we have heard," then said the clock, "it is imperative that we should come to some conclusion upon this matter without further delay; and that is best done, in my opinion, not by listening longer to the poker or the tongs, or any one else who makes speeches, but by consulting the canary himself. And as there is no need for me to send any one to prison, where they are all more or less already, I adjudicate that the canary be consulted at once."

"The canary is fast asleep, my lud," said the poker; "and, unless you are a fire, or a murderer, or a policeman, or a fractious child, you cannot waken people up suddenly, even to show you are interested in them; it would be considered rude."

"*I* can, though," said a voice in Court.

It was a quill pen who spoke. She was tired of writing prim little notes (it was so long since she had had to answer the love letters), and quite used to settling accounts, so up she rose to settle this discussion.

Light as the feather she was she flew to the cage, and, poking herself through its bars, gently pricked the canary's head.

So the same little slumberous head came, ruffled, from under the wing to ask, as the Judge had done some time before him, "What is the matter?"

Back flew the quill to the table, while the tongs explained to the canary all that had happened.

When he understood how nearly everything in the room had been brought into the discussion, he opened his beak in a wide yawn, and stretched out his wings, for he had been most rudely wakened out of his sleep, and then he said—

"The tongs says truly. I am most melancholy, while I sing cheerfully enough, because I have been sad at heart ever since I was put into this miserable cage. It is only the recollection of joyfulness which lifts and thrills my song—the remembrance of what I used to feel when I was free."

"Tack!" said the Judge; "that concludes the case. And my advice to all present is, in the future, do not judge by appearances only, for those who do so are frequently found to be in the wrong."

THE FAIRY-RING.

N the country sometimes, in the wide fields or sheltered vales, you may come across large rings of greenest grass on the sward, known as "fairy-rings." They are plainly to be seen, because they appear such a very bright green, compared with the rest of the grass that grows thereabouts; and they vary in size and in shape a little, but are always more or less circular.

They are to be met with often in the Isle of Man, that fairy haunt; and if you were to ask there what fairy-rings are, you would be told by the Manx people that they mark the place whereon the fairies dance on summer nights.

The grass is greener and more beautiful after a fairy dance.

Well, we mortals can hardly understand that! We only wear out the carpets or scratch the polished floor when *we* dance!

But then one always hears that fairies are such very different creatures.

Where they come from nobody seems to know—and nobody ever knew—because nobody looked to see just at the right time!

Some old women have searched bread-mugs for them, and not succeeded in finding them; but what of that? Who but a half-blind old woman could hope to find a fairy in a bread-mug?

Some old grandfathers have chosen to suspect the chimneys of being a daytime resting-place for them; but, as if fairies could care to rest upon soot!

Little girls peep into the Canterbury bells and foxgloves for them; but, if fairies are of different sizes and shapes—as we have reason to suspect they are—these would not accommodate them all. Besides, would not the bees find them sadly in the way when they came there to fetch honey? And the noise a bee makes buzzing about its work would seem like a dreadful alarum to a tender fairy's sensitive ears, one would think!

The truth is, nobody ever knew where they put themselves in the daytime, any more than how they appear at night. So some boys say they "don't believe in fairies," and some middle-aged people give up hope of ever finding any.

Never mind! Every one who is not so conceited as to think he knows everything (which nobody can know in this wonderful world) is sure some good, and fine, and delicate Power is hidden away somewhere in the Universe, always ready to help to cheer the good, and thwart evil; to conjure up hope in desponding hearts with pleasant surprises; and treat kind people to the kind turns they, in time past, have done for others—some Power magical enough to beautify whatever it touches.

Well, let it be called whatsoever you will, it may be due to the fairies!

But the mystery of where they put themselves in the daytime is ever unsolved.

We suspect they utterly change their sub-
stance, as the dewdrops do; that they are
distilled into and out of the sunshine or moon-
shine. Who can tell?

More wonderful things happen every day
than any one takes notice of; and, may be,
they go to the sun in the daytime, and come
back by the moon at night, without a thought
of rest at all, as sunshine itself does. Indeed,
might not fairies be condensed through suit-
able conditions and the presence of moonlight,
just as easily as are dewdrops through the
absence of sunshine and clouds?

Who can tell? Natural processes we take
for granted—the smoke tumbling up in the
still summer air instead of down; the hoar
frost making transformation scenes of beautiful tracery in a single night, are just as wonderful as fairies and fairy workmanship. Only
just because we have found out something
about the conditions which produce these, we

call them *natural*, and think no more about them.

Well, let us learn all we can about these natural wonders ; for they ought to teach us how multitudinous are the powers at work in nature, and how vast is the sphere of possibilities there; not to conclude, as ignorant little boys and girls do, that because we " don't believe " in anything, that therefore it does not exist.

If you were to tell a mole " the sun is shining " when all the flowers were rejoicing in it, and all the little ducklings were taking to the water for the first time—pricking up their new little feathers because of it, and everything in the meadows was springing towards it ; the mole, from the bottom of his subterraneous passage and the depth of his blindness might sturdily assert that he " didn't believe you."

But, mark you this, *the sun would be shining all the same !*

So, whenever you hear people say there

are no fairies, remember this mole; and
good fairies may still exist for you in spite
of the poor, blind people who cannot see
them !

At any rate we are going to have a good
look at them to-night, you and I, and a mutual
friend. We are going to try and find out
where they come from and whither they go,
and what they do and how they do it; and
altogether satisfy our curiosity about them.
It is June. And we came to the Isle of Man
last Saturday; just in time to buy the rhubarb
leaves full of strawberries which they sell on
the Douglas promenade.

We have stayed a day or two here, and
made excursions to different parts of the
island; but now we are quite determined to eat
no more strawberries, no, nor enjoy anything
else whatever until we have made a grand
excursion to see the fairies.

We came across one of the fairy-rings in a
pretty vale yesterday morning, where we had
driven some distance inland; so we shall visit

it again to-night when the moon is up, and enjoy ourselves.

Ah! shall we be fortunate enough to find the fairies at their dance; or shall we only prove ourselves to be "moles" that cannot see?

Time will show. The night is beautiful. As we leave the sea its waves are lulling each other and caressing the shore, and the magnificent moon rises; the whole of the heavenly vault is irradiated by it.

Just the night for the fairy distillery to work! Surely we shall see fairies to-night!

Half-an-hour's drive along the moonlit roads and the man pulls up. We get out of the carriage and leave him to smoke his pipe and meditate upon what has induced us to take a drive in the middle of the night, when his fare is doubled.

After a few minutes' walk we see the roofless chapel which no one could satisfactorily finish, because the energetic fairies would come to pull the roof off again directly it was put on;

and then, turning down a field-path to the
left, we find the ring again.

A rock rises behind the velvet sward where
the ring is, a waterfall dances down not far
away, and a stream runs round two sides of
it; all this is plainly discernible in the moonlight.

Somehow we begin to feel uncanny. It is
close upon midnight; but for our watches
we should not have known that though, as
we are far from the sound of the clock's
striking.

Cowering under the rock behind a bush,
where we can see without being seen, we await
what shall be revealed.

There is no fear of our falling asleep; the
only fear is that our mutual friend will imagine
something before she really sees anything at
all; because she is rather an uncertain, nervous
person, the sort of person who says, "What is
that?" in a tone of alarm if a cinder drop
upon the hearthstone, when anyone else,
hearing that same sound, would recognise it as

E

the old original sound which a cinder always did and always will make upon dropping from the grate to the hearth.

In fact she is not at all the sort of person you or I would have chosen to have with us on an uncanny expedition of this kind; the truth is she invited herself, and we have long since made up our minds to trust to our own senses rather than her exclamations.

So far she has not uttered one. Presently we hear something peculiar: it is a mournful twirl of a sound that you and I at once recognise as the melancholy cry of an owl; but our friend jumps decidedly, and breathlessly looks to us for explanation.

We soothe her agitation by explaining it in a whisper, and bid her watch the ring.

We all do so most intently for some time; but nothing unusual is to be seen.

We feel a good deal though, for the place is damp, and however beautiful moonlight is, damp and cramp interfere with the enjoyment of it.

We are just making confession of this under our breath to each other, when a delicious sound fills and thrills the distance. It rises and falls, dies, then melodiously and generously breaks out again—like a never to be forgotten joy, in a rush of memory.

Cramp and everything else are forgotten as we listen, spellbound. In the middle of all this you and I suddenly clasp each other's hands, for there, as though ushered in by this fluting prelude, are one, two, four, half-a dozen streaks of light, settling themselves round and over the fairy-ring. They hover in the air, sometimes seem to go out, but generally reappear, just as you miss them.

Oh! dear, this is delightful!

These must be fairy-lights. We hope the nightingale will go on singing, for this seems to bring them.

"What's that?" our friend, who has gone marble pale at this sight, may well now exclaim, for somehow there has come a rainbow-like shimmering of beautiful colouring into the ring, you cannot tell how; but it rises above the surrounding lights, then sinks again. And now—yes, at last, here are *the fairies!*

Beautiful, airy, fleet little beings, bounding about, some of them, like india-rubber, flitting about; others like butterflies, dressed as the flowers are, and graceful as they, constantly vanishing and reappearing in a bewildering manner. How long will this go on?

Ah! now they are settled and visible indeed, looking positively tangible. It is with the greatest difficulty I prevent you from putting out your hand to take and kiss one sweet little fay. She has flown very near the bush we crouch behind, and sits upon the frond of a fern. She is about six inches in height. Two of the tiniest petals from a tea-rose, tilted up and curved, crown her hair; her pretty short skirts are nothing but more of these fragrant petals; and, dear me! how very curious, her wings somehow absorb the moonlight, so as to appear green, like the delicate leaves from a rose tree.

For a moment she watches the others, pensively, then falls to flirting with a glow-worm! He was shining most desperately close by, in the hope of attracting her attention.

But who would have thought of her flirting with a glow-worm, and such an airy fairy, too, as she is!

One would have expected her to flirt with the glow without the worm.

Meanwhile something is happening to the fairy-ring. The little fay gets fluttered and flies back.

The Queen, the Queen, THE QUEEN, has come.

Alas! we never saw how. As usual, we were not looking at the right time. However, there she is now, and transcendently lovely!

What a change, too, has taken place in the fairy-ring. A peaceful pool has appeared in the centre of it.

The Queen's feet rest upon lily-leaves. She is throned upon a crescent moon.

Tiny stars of golden light are fixed around her brow. Her perfect form is draped with a wreathing pure white cloudlet. Her glorious hair falls waving about her; while all around her and above the ring, settles a concentrated power of golden light, which looks like the essence of joy.

Tiny doves, that seem to tell of the peace which springs where the Queen reigns, fly about her, and she carries a wand of pure crystal in her hand; it is a sign of the strength and purity of her sway.

On her beautiful face is set the expression of a noble purpose, and her eyes are liquid with pity and love.

As she rises and raises the wand in greeting, the air becomes suddenly melodious, and the fairies spring and fling themselves together in a wild dance of joy around their Queen. All the time the sweet hubbub of spiritual sound continues, the musicians thus invoked remain invisible; and although the theme is beyond our ken, the fairies might be part of it, so completely do their movement express unison with it.

In staccato passages they fall asunder, each separately making obeisance to the Queen, but when the sustained rhythm returns, they fling together again and, with unanimous and continuous action, move in a ring as before.

Watching the fairy dance we forget every-thing else, even the nightingale's singing. How long we crouch in this wrapt attention we cannot tell; but the sound of a cock crow is heard, and heigh! ho! in a trice all are gone! vanished!

Not even a lock of the fairy Queen's hair, or a petal from a fairy crown is left behind; and but for the corroboration from the three pairs of eyes, and the three pairs of ears of the three wide-awake persons cowering behind the bushes, we might have thought we had been dreaming.

But we all three know that we have not been even to sleep! So there the matter rests.

We walk quietly back to the carriage, still quite overpowered by the beauty of the scene we have just witnessed; and after that when

other peeple tell us they "don't believe" in
fairies, we pity them, and class them as moles
who cannot see, while our minds wander back
to a certain summer night, to a romantic
island in the middle of the Irish Sea, and to
the beautiful fairy dance we so distinctly saw
there.

And whenever we see the green, green
grass that marks a fairy-ring, we wish that
we ourselves were more like fairies who
beautify what they touch. And we think that
perhaps if we had such a noble purpose and
pity, and love at heart, as shone from the
face of that beautiful fairy Queen, the glad-
some actions we should then be able to do,
would prove as great a blessing to those
around us, as did the fairy dance to the
fairy-ring.

THE CUCKOO.

NE fine day Mrs. Thrush, who lived in a beautiful nest built on the forked branch of a tree, was very angry, and this was the reason of it.

When she came home from flying about and picking up food on lawns miles distant, what should she find but a perfect stranger, a large cuckoo, sitting in her nest as comfortably as though it belonged to him!

"You might have knocked me down with a *wren's* feather," she told her husband afterwards, in describing the incident to him; "I was so taken aback; I had heard of, but never seen such impudence before!"

Oddly enough, a few days afterwards, Mrs. Blackbird had the same tale to tell her husband.

"I thought at first it was you, my dear,

carefully keeping the eggs warm, having returned home before me," she said, "but when
I got near enough to see, I found to my
disgust it was a horrid *brown* cuckoo, filling
up the nest as though it were his own, and
sitting on my eggs, too!"

Mr. Blackbird was naturally indignant when
he heard this, and very justly remarked:
"When we want a nurse, my dear, we can
advertise for one, but no bird can submit to
such an intrusion twice."

Now if the blackbirds could but have heard,
Mr. and Mrs. Starling were holding almost the
same conversation in another part of the
forest.

In fact, not one pair of birds, but many a
pair, in every part of the forest which was
frequented by a cuckoo, had the same com-
plaint to make.

So a few weeks later, when Mrs. Thrush
had returned home again, again to find that
impertinent cuckoo sitting in her nest, Mr.
Thrush took action.

He called a conference together of all the birds of the forest, to be held in the largest oak tree there, when the sun should be high in the heavens, the subject of discussion to be, " How we are to punish that cuckoo?"

And he left word at very nearly all the nests in the forest; and even the owls and the nightingales consented to come when they heard what the discussion was to be about, though none of these liked going about in the daytime. The owls were so blind then, and the nightingales so tired after their midnight singing.

When the time came, therefore, all the birds were gathered together in the oak tree, and you never heard such a chattering as there was in your life.

Each bird wanted to tell his own particular instance of the cuckoo's impertinent entrance into his own nest, but no bird wanted to hear his neighbour's experience; and as they all persisted in talking at once, no single one got a hearing, till the lark sank down from

above to tell them their noise was "disgrace-
ful."

"Get a chairman, or, to speak more appro-
priately, a *bough*man," she said, "to preside
over the meeting and keep the peace."

But this suggestion only caused more
wrangling still, for the birds could not de-
cide who should be placed in that enviable
position, the top of the tree; because each
had a secret conviction that he himself could
best fill the post, and this made him object
to every other suggestion made.

So the whole day passed in useless talk.

The sun was obliged to go down before they
had done; and the oak tree thought, as he
felt himself laden with chattering birds, that,
whatever their business might be, it could not
be so objectionably important as they themselves were. All that day they arrived at no
conclusion in the matter, and all the next they
would have still wrangled; but at noon the
forest became gloomy; the sunlight disappeared; a thunderstorm came on.

This utterly frightened and scattered the birds.

The lightning flashed, the thunder roared, and the tree swayed to and fro as the rain came down in torrents, and every forest creature hid itself until the face of nature should smile again. ·

When the weather did clear, and Mr. Thrush was able to fly back to his wife, anxious to tell her about the conference—from which domestic duties had detained her—he was much astonished to find a great disturbance going on in one of the trees near where his way lay.

Several of the birds that had been at the conference were chirping about in a very concerned manner indeed; and he was still more astonished when he learnt the reason of it, which Mr. and Mrs. Starling rushed out to tell him.

They said, " Just when the storm cleared we made for home, because it suddenly occurred to us that all the time we were talking in the oak tree the cuckoo might be sitting in our nest. And, sure enough, when we got back, there he had been; but, to our dismay, we found that both he and our nest had been struck to the earth by the lightning!"

Mr. Thrush looked at the ground as the starling spoke, and there lay the poor cuckoo —dead; the nest broken in pieces about him.

This was the sight which made the birds so concerned.

They took the poor, sad-looking, stark little body away, and laid it near a quiet stream, and covered it with leaves. Each little bird brought one in his beak as a tribute of forgiveness, and then they all cried—as well as they could—and felt very mournful.

Indeed, such numbers of birds came from all parts of the forest when they heard of the cuckoo's fate, that the gathering of forgiveness at the stream was even more numerously attended than the conference which met to condemn him had been.

Night was falling in as the owl brought his, the last tribute, to the cuckoo's funeral, so perhaps that was the reason he was able to see so clearly just then, for he said :

"We, who have so many faults of our own, and are vain and quarrelsome, forgive you your fault against us, O cuckoo! And we are not surprised that the avenging power which destroyed you destroyed at the same time one of our nests ; for which of us does not deserve punishment for some fault or other!"

Then the owl laid his leaf penitently upon the dead cuckoo's tail and flew solemnly away; as, in due time, did they all.

And after the poor cuckoo was killed by the storm, the birds in that forest never again found fault with each other so readily as they had done before.

FORGET-ME-NOTS.

"YOU are very mild-looking and very blue!" said a frog, looking at a number of forget-me-nots that were growing on the outskirts of a pond out of which he had just jumped.

The forget-me-nots were much too tranquil to be disturbed into replying by a personal remark of that kind; but a duck that was swimming about near took up the cudgels at once.

"Quack!" she said; "well, you are neither yourself, but a yellow, bulging, jumping, croaking person, whose eyes look as though they might drop out of your head any minute, and get lost in the water!"

"Humph!" exclaimed the frog, "it's no affair of yours; I wasn't speaking to you, but thinking aloud. I suppose people may think aloud if they like, mayn't they?"

" Quack!" said the duck, "if they do they must take the consequences; and the consequences of thinking aloud are, that other people will overhear them, and take them to task for their thoughts."

" Humph!" returned the frog, "you are ready enough with your word! Where do you come from?" But he received no answer to this, for the only part of the duck left above water to give any answer was its tail—head and body were lost to sight under water.

" There's never any conversation to be got with a duck," the frog grumbled to himself; " I've noticed that before. They just throw out the first remark that comes into their heads, and then turn tail uppermost to avoid your reply."

But the duck's head had been up listening to him for some moments, and she quacked in, " On the contrary, we are generally up in time to hear the tail end of what you are talking about."

The frog was startled, because he did not know the duck's head was above water again.

"Come on land," at last he said, gruffly, "if you want to have it out with me, then I shall know which end of you will be uppermost without keeping an eye upon you all the time."

But the duck knew she had the best of it on the water, so she swam away; and there was nothing left for the frog to talk to but the mild, blue forget-me-nots.

He jumped about and croaked a good deal, hoping to attract their attention in that way; but as they took no notice of him whatever, he began, "Humph! if I may make so bold as to inquire, what are you thinking about all day long? If you would think aloud, as other people do sometimes, it would make the after-noon pleasanter!"

The duck had once more come by, so she put in here, "Quack! that would depend upon what their thoughts were. I doubt if *your* thoughts would make any afternoon the plea-santer," and before the frog could retaliate to this disagreeable remark, she was topsy turvy again.

But all at once one of the forget-me-nots began thinking aloud for the benefit of that jumping, bulging, yellow creature the frog; and this was what she thought:

"We rise from the waters
 To greet the fair Shower,
For we are the daughters,
 Born in glad hour,
Of Earth and the Sky."

Here, however, the frog interrupted her. " If you are the daughters, which are the sons?" he asked.

"It does not follow that there are sons because there are daughters," the forget-me-not said gently; "we have no brothers that we know of."

"Humph!" said the frog, "I thought it did, that's all. But when I come to look at you, you forget-me-nots, you do look so much alike, I expect you are all twins, ay?" he ended, interrogatively.

" Since there are so many of us alike, twins we cannot be," again the forget-me-not gently corrected.

" Then I expect you all came to life in a batch like crocodiles' eggs ! " concluded the frog ; " go on."

And the forget-me-not continued :

> " Ah ! fondly we yearn for
> Our father, the Sky ;
> The Earth, our dear mother,
> We always are nigh ;
> For our father we sigh."

" Better do something else, it's no good sighing," interrupted the frog ; " your father, the sky, will never hear that, he's so far off ! Try jumping. You would get nearer to him if you were to jump as I do."

" We don't wish to leave our mother, the Earth, though," objected the forget-me-not in prose. " As it is, we can *feel* her at our roots, though we never see much of her, but if we were to jump we should have to come up by the roots, separate ourselves from her, and

never reach him, our father the Sky, after all ;
but fall back most certainly to die."

" That would be a pity," said the frog ; "but
I can't see that a little jumping should hurt
anyone. It's the only exercise I ever take—
except swimming of course"—he added
hastily. "I have a good deal of that; but I
find that jumping always does me good."
And thereupon he jumped about to prove what
he said.

The forget-me-not watched him, but said
nothing; for she had now found out that the
frog was one of those people who judge the
whole world by their own small experience,
and disbelieve other people's, whatever that
may be; but one of the tiniest forget-me-nots
put in : "We never take any exercise at all.
Nothing does us so much good as standing
still and looking up to our dear father, the
Sky."

Just then the duck, who had returned un-
perceived by them and been standing tail
uppermost for some time near, burst in with,

"I, on the contrary, get most good by looking *down;* and that is the simple reason why I do it so often."

And the next instant she went head first down again.

Now these interruptions all made the frog angry, for the duck kept taking him by surprise, and the frog was just the sort of person to feel decidedly irritated when taken by surprise.

"What a creature that duck is for joining uninvited into the conversation!" he observed, testily. "I never saw her like!"

But the forget-me-not here began to think aloud again :

> "The Shower will carry
> A message for me."

"Humph! that *is* nonsense," burst in the frog. "How can it? Such nonsense! I never heard of a shower doing anything but coming down and splashing upon stones ; and since there are no stones in the sky, it can't even do that up there! How will it carry your message? How can it ever get back *up* into the sky again at all, let alone carry anybody's messages there?"

The forget-me-not's thoughts, however, had been so upset by these constant interruptions that she did not reply at all to this question.

"Ho! ho! *you* can interrupt other people when they are thinking aloud, I hear," again burst in the duck, who was round unexpectedly again as usual; "I thought you didn't like it yourself, and that that was why you found fault with me a minute or two ago! What a fellow you are! And as ignorant of the shower and its ways, too, as can be! I suppose you think everyone croaks when they send or take a message, as you yourself do! Well, you are very much mistaken, Mr. Frog; and, mark my words, these forget-me-nots know a great deal more than you do about some things."

"Well," rejoined the frog, crestfallen under the duck's sharp attack, "I merely ask *how* is the shower to carry a message to any-one?"

"You listen to the forget-me-not without interrupting, who knows so much more than you or I do, for the matter of that, though she does nothing but stand still and look up all day long, and you shall hear," said the duck.

The forget-me-not was still silent, however, so they listened in vain.

"Quack! you see what you've done now," said the duck (who it seemed could remain still and horizontal when no one was going to make a retort); "you've exhausted the kindness of our dear little forget-me-not, who never by any chance loses her temper. It's a disgrace! Now you may listen and listen, but you'll grow none the wiser, because the forget-me-not will not think aloud for your benefit any longer. She'll think all the rest of the time to herself."

And, having quite aired her sentiments, the duck dived again, leaving the frog thoroughly disconsolate and ashamed of himself.

" Humph ! " was his mental note, " I wish I
hadn't been such a fool. There is something
in what that duck says, after all ! Perhaps,"
he pondered, " by putting so much of herself
out of sight directly she's said anything, she
makes her remarks more impressive. I'll try
the effect of that plan upon the forget-me-not ;
for I want to hear how the shower can carry a
message to the sky."

" I am afraid you think I was rude, forget-
me-not ! " he exclaimed, and, plunging into
the edge of the pond, he endeavoured to stand
upon his head by sticking it into the soft mud
at the bottom of the pond edge, and kicking his
legs out of the surface of the water violently
behind.

But the forget-me-not took no notice of
what the frog was doing ; and when, after
having been very uncomfortable, he regained
his natural position to wonder what effect his
imitation of the duck had wrought, it was to
find three dragon-flies hovering above his head,
laughing at him. All their wings were shaking

with laughter, and they had gradually been coming nearer and nearer the surface of the water, and nearer his struggling limbs, in that tremulous, tentative, dropping hover with which dragon-flies vary their darting flight, to see if it really could be their old friend, the frog, behaving so madly!

"Hollo! he! he!" they exclaimed; "then it *is* you? We thought we recognised something about the hind legs; but what was the matter?"

"Did you have a fit?" asked one.

"Or had something you were catching caught you?" asked another.

"Or perhaps you really had stuck fast in the mud?" cried the third.

"He! he!" laughed they all; "it really was a sight to see you standing on your head in the mud."

"Humph!" said the frog, again crestfallen and ashamed of himself, and very much taken by surprise and annoyed, "it's no affair of yours. I suppose people may kick out of the water if they like, mayn't they?"

" Yes, yes," said all the little dragon-flies;
" do it again—we like to see you! We dart
about a good deal over the pond, but we never
before saw anything so amusing as a frog
behaving like that."

" Unless it had got its head fast in the
weeds," added one.

But the duck had been round for some time
unobserved, and now put in, " Quack! people
may do ridiculous things if they like, of course,
but they must take the consequences if they do ;
and the consequence of doing a foolish thing
is, that other people will laugh at them. I was
at the other side of the pond, and saw there
was something going on here, so back I came
at once, and I see what he has been doing.
The frog has just been rude to the forget-
me-nots," she explained, turning to the dragon-
flies, " and I daresay he thought to make it up
by imitating me because they are great friends
of mine. Quack! quack! I hate such work!"

" He! he!" laughed all the little dragon-
flies; " who would have thought this of our

friend the frog? How was he rude to the forget-me-nots, Mrs. Duck?"

"Well," replied the duck, "she was thinking aloud on purpose to make the afternoon a little the pleasanter for him, as he had asked her to do, and he needs must interrupt her to say he didn't believe her! I consider that rude, don't you? I call it rude to interrupt one at all, but to interrupt any one to say she is talking nonsense when she is telling the truth; I call that *very* rude, don't you?"

And the duck quite forgot to turn topsy-turvy, she was so indignant, while all the little dragon-flies called out—

"He! he! very rude, *very* rude."

And the frog was covered with confusion, which he manifested by looking yellower and more bulging than ever, and by his eyes becoming more prominent than before, while his skin and limbs seemed to be paralysed with fear.

And just at this very awkward moment,

what should come to turn away attention from the unhappy frog, who was suffering so acutely from the condemnation he richly deserved, but the forget-me-not, thinking aloud again, as though nothing whatever had happened to interrupt her! So that, just as the frog thoroughly realised how rude he had been to contradict her—how foolish to imitate the duck in order to make a better impression upon her, and how ignorant he was about the shower, and about exercise not being good for forget-me-nots, and everything else in the world except jumping and croaking, the for-get-me-not forgave him, and went on thinking aloud, just as though nothing disagreeable had happened—

> " So, nightly returning
>   As vapour on high,
> The shower our yearning
>   Tells to the blue sky:
> Who brightens with pleasure
>   And rare joy above,
> To learn of his treasure,
>   His dear daughter's love."

"And the thought of the shower's carrying that message does cheer us wonderfully," concluded the forget-me-not, in prose.

"I am obliged to you for thinking aloud," said the frog; "I am much obliged," for, while listening to the end of the forget-me-not's thoughts, he had recovered his self-possession; and he felt happier now that he had heard how the shower did ascend into the sky again. He was surprised it did not jump.

Even the duck could see that a desirable change had come over him, and remarked, "I am glad you appreciate the forget-me-nots at last, Mr. Frog! Quack!"

"He! he! so are we—so are we!" chimed in the dragon-flies, their wings shaking with satisfaction this time. "We are very fond of all the forget-me-nots."

"Humph!" continued the frog; "there is something in being mild, after all, if it prevents them from being so irritable as I am!" and he jumped as he made this great confession. "And as for their being *blue*," he concluded, "humph! that very fact should have told me long ago that they were related to the sky; they are exactly the same colour as he."

And with this he jumped away, the dragon-flies darted off, the duck stood tail uppermost in the water for so long, naturally and happily, that one almost despaired of ever seeing her head again; and all was peace on the pond once more, as the blue forget-me-nots con-tinued to gaze up to the blue, blue sky.

THE LAD'S HOUSE.

HE particular person I want to tell you about to-day was a lad who lived once upon a time in this flower-be-sprinkled world, when curious events were always happening.

From the beginning he was in comfortable circumstances, for his father, who was very rich, made him the handsome present of a house directly he was born; in fact, the very house the lad was born in the father made over to him for life.

"It is rather small at present," said his father, when the lad was old enough to understand; "but don't be anxious on that score, for when you grow it will grow too, so that it will last you your lifetime; and, as it is a moveable house, you can take it about with you wherever you go. And prize it; for if this comes to grief, I cannot provide you with another like it."

Then the lad's mother showed him over it.

There were several stories, a great many passages, staircases, and two or three chambers in it; and the walls of almost all the rooms and passages were red—a deep terra-cotta colour.

At the very top of all, however, was one room, which had cream-coloured walls and a skylight. This was the study, the most interesting of all the rooms in the house, and there was a little private chapel near it.

Of course, too, there were a front and a back door, and windows to the house.

Now, although most of the rooms—the kitchen and dining-room, for instance—were furnished when the lad was born, the study and the little private chapel were not.

"Those," said his mother, "you will have to furnish bit by bit yourself, as you grow up. I will help you to begin," she added.

Then she gave him a beautiful image of a saint to put upon the altar in his chapel. And she taught him to sing and to play upon the organ there.

The lad was truly happy for many years; and indeed he might well be, for his life was a very enjoyable one.

In the winter time, when the soft snow fell, making the face of Nature so pure and beautiful, he, with other lads, would rush out into it, and, pressing it into hard balls, they would fling it at each other in great enjoyment. Or he would pause in crossing the fields to notice how very black the uncovered parts of the tree-branches looked, and how fascinating was their tracery against the background of white snow or blue sky.

As for the soft, luxurious, pure snow, which the wind had drifted around in heaps, he felt he would like to roll in them as the dogs did. They scampered over the hard, frozen roads, then they rolled about in the snow-drifts, enjoying themselves to the full.

"Winter is delightful!" the boy thought; and he looked forward to skating all the year round.

And how about spring, when that drew near? Well, that he thought delightful, too.

Then he could ramble over the meadows, and find the early flowers, and peep into the hedges and the trees where the birds built, to see how many pretty eggs had been laid, or race with the skittish, easily frightened lambs.

Then he could gaze from the hills at the advancing April shower, as it came gradually nearer and nearer, as a veil might move among the hills and valleys, watering the tender shoots that were springing to light, and softening the bursting buds.

And when summer came round, Nature seemed to him even more delightful still. Then there was wading to be had in the cool, clear river near the stepping-stones, when the air was so full of warmth that even the tops of these stones themselves were warmed by the sun in the midst of the clear, cool water.

Then the wild flowers were blowing abundantly in the fragrant meadows among the sweet, tall grass.

He collected many of the flowers, learnt their names, and stored them in his study; and he wandered at ease through the shady, quiet woods.

To add to all this happiness, one summer, after some years had passed away, he found in the shady wood sweet Lizzette.

She lived there in her little house with an aunt.

And as autumn came on turning the leaves to gold and ripening the fruit, the friendship of these two ripened into love.

The nightingale said, "I have watched the youth and the maid walk out together in the evening; and then sit, as the sun set, on a heathery knoll, and though the air around was soft and cool, they blushed with love's excitement.

"It will be a match," concluded the nightingale.

" They will pair, they will pair," cooed the ringdove.

Thus the lad grew up into a tall youth; and, sure enough, his house grew with him, just as his father had said it would do; it enlarged of its own accord in the most convenient manner possible.

"It is really a capital house," said the youth to himself when he considered this; "I am, as I ought to be, thankful for it."

And as he grew still older he began to understand that when he met Lizzette his pulse beat with a quickened life, and that, when he did not meet her, life seemed flat and the world dull.

And all the grasses and flowers in the wood and on the hillside, where the two used to meet, whispered, " They love."

However, about this time a very strange thing happened to that wonderful house in which the youth lived. I will try to describe it to you.

Hitherto he had deemed it the most con-

venient house in the world, as we know; now
he began to think it just the opposite; and for
this reason.

At nights now, when he retired to rest,
instead of enjoying that profound and un-
broken rest which had always before been his,
he was kept awake by a most bitter experience.

This was what now happened.

As the youth lay in bed, lights began to
dither and dance around his chamber, and hot
air to seethe about him, till, when midnight
had struck, from a trap-door at the end of one
of the passages would emerge a strange figure
—the figure of a man, but deformed into a
demon of glowing flame.   Entering at the
closed door of the bedchamber, this form
would advance towards the bed with glowing
eyes, and bending over the stricken youth
would half consume him with a terrible heat
and horror.

Night after night the unfortunate youth
went through this dreadful experience, with
occasional weeks of respite interspersed, and

he became worn and pale as a shadow; for
the house which he could not get rid of,
when his father had made it over to him for
life, was haunted; and in consequence of
this the youth's life became a burden to
him.

"He is pining, he is pining," cooed the
ringdoves with quick sympathy, as he passed
through the woods in the fresh morning air
looking scared and wan.

And in truth the youth was grieving at
heart, for he thought, "I cannot ask sweet
Lizzette to be my wife, I, who am haunted by
a demon ghost! I must first get rid of the
demon before I can tell her that I love her
even. Alas! that it should be so; for I do
love her with all my heart."

Then he wandered about, and gazed at her
window from afar; and puzzled his brains as
to how he should get rid of his demon visitor;
but he never once thought of consulting
Lizzette herself.

And time passed on. Just now, when they

met, the maid could scarcely understand her
lover's behaviour, for he was constrained and
silent, and never said—though he held her
hand so long at parting—"Will you be my
wife?"

"Ernest does *not* love me, after all,"
thought sweet Lizzette; and the tears that
rose to her eyes were almost checked by the
indignant question, "Then why did he woo
me?"

About this time the owl and the nightingale
had a talk together.

"The young man grows pale and ill," said
the nightingale; "the ringdove says he is
dying of love for the maid."

"Tee-whit, tee-who!" rejoined the owl,
most attentively.

"The maid sits lonely, and as she listens
to my song her heart swells within her. If
she could but follow her thoughts, she herself would melt into the presence of the youth,
as cloudlets melt towards the full and golden
moon."

" Tee-whoo ! '' again rejoined the owl.

"Why do they not marry?" abruptly inquired the nightingale.

"You see, there is something in the way,"
the owl replied.

He then told the nightingale all about the
demon who haunted the youth at night; for the
owl had watched and seen all through the
window several times.

The nightingale was very quiet after she
heard this: she was thinking her own little
thoughts; then she flew away.

She flew till she reached the window of the
feverish youth, which was open, and, hopping
inside, witnessed the whole scene for herself, her
little beak twittering with fright the while. And
when, after the ghastly spectre's retirement, the
youth lay still and exhausted, the nightingale
picked up an open letter from his dressing-
table, and again flew off in another direction.

This time it was to the maid's window that
she flew, and, dropping the letter upon the
window-sill, she poured forth from a neigh-

bouring branch such a volume of song as brought the maid near to listen.

And there lay the letter. The maid saw it and took it in.

A dried flower was pinned upon one side of it, one which Lizzette recognised, for she had herself given it to Ernest a month before, and beside the flower was written in his handwriting these words—

"Precious gift from a tender hand—
  A true, sweet heart that holds my own,
Would that I could, as oft I've planned,
  Take that dear heart as my life's throne!
Alas! a fierce ghost glides between,
And scatters all my hopeful dream."

When Lizzette had read these words a blush brightened her face, and, as she pressed the letter to her lips, she murmured,

"Dear Ernest, I am yours, since you do love me, and you are mine; and no demon shall torment you if I can help it."

The next day she started for the heart of the forest, thinking all the time that Ernest himself must have placed those lines upon her window-sill the night before.

Now the reason she went to the heart of the forest was this: An old grandame lived there, Witch Griffin, who was so old and so wise, she knew nearly everything that other people did not know; and whenever the people of that country side were in a difficulty, they went to consult Witch Griffin.

"She will tell me how to help my beloved," thought Lizzette; so she walked away fast all day, that she might reach the witch before nightfall. At last, when she was tired, she sat down to rest for a little while under the trees.

The sun set, and the squirrels were chattering above her; but Lizzette could not understand what they said.

"Where is she going?" asked one.

"To the witch," returned another. "I have watched her most of the day, and she has been going straight towards the witch's cave."

"I wish she wouldn't sit upon my nuts!"

chimed in a third, his bright eyes twinkling with anxiety; "she is upon the very spot where I have hidden a heap of them away for next winter."

"Never mind," said a fourth, "she won't crack them."

"Well, if she isn't quick, she will miss what she came for," said the first, whisking up his tail preparatory to retiring for the night, "for Witch Griffin goes out at moonrise, as we all know."

But Lizzette could not understand them, so she rose in a leisurely manner to continue her journey; and, just as the beams from the risen moon fell, soft and mild, into the heart of the forest, she caught sight of the witch's cave.

A deep dell, sunk among the trees, led to it, as Lizzette knew well.

At first, as she approached it, she thought a fringe of moonlight hung round the mouth of the cave, but soon she discovered it was a fringe of glow-worms which illumined its outline.

As she paused before entering this gloomy
dell, a sensation of awe crept over her for a
time. However, just as she had nerved herself to enter it, and was looking intently
before her in order to do so, a dark object
shot out from the entrance, obliterating the
light from some of the glow-worm fringe for a
moment, to appear the next, clearly defined
against the moonlit sky. It was plainly Witch
Griffin upon a broomstick; she was evidently
off, and away for the night.

At seeing the object of her search thus
elude her, after so long and toilsome a journey, Lizzette was deeply disappointed.

Involuntarily she called after the witch; but
so swift was the locomotive power in the
broomstick, that by the time Lizzette had
uttered a sound it and the witch were quite
out of sight.

Tears of disappointment rose to the
maiden's eyes; but thinking that, at all
events, she would enter the cave and wait
for Witch Griffin's return, after having come

so far to see her, even though she had to sit up all night for it, Lizzette approached the cave in order to do so.

Feeling about in the dark, she at length found two or three ledges of rock, by means of which she managed to climb into the mouth of the cave.

There she sat down, wishing that glow-worm light were brighter, her heart beating with fright, as she felt all kinds of little bones, and queer odds and ends upon the floor where she stretched her hands about to feel her way. At last she discerned a faint light at the far end of the cave. Evidently it issued from an inner sanctum.

Lizzette at once made her way towards this, finding as she did so that the cave she was in narrowed in this direction to a passage. At the end of this passage a blank wall faced her; but to the right, where the light fell through, was an opening.

Lizzette looked through, and started with pleasure and surprise as a lovely sight met her eyes.

She had peeped in through a sort of natural window in the dome of a huge cave, which stretched away far below, in the centre of which softly beamed an indescribable sun. Rays from this bathed the cave in a flood of soft light. The sides of it were covered with the most delicate flowers, moss, and vegetation. The flowers were more delicate, the moss more velvety, than any to be met with on the earth's surface, though they were similar to these in kind.

But especially the light fell immediately below upon a small lake of magical water, where ethereal water-lilies and slender reeds rose. And a dainty, almost transparent, cloudlet floated between this sun and this water.

On the cloudlet reclined the greatest wonder the cave contained—a beautiful winged child, with wide open, dreamy eyes.

Lizzette gazed entranced till a sigh of joy escaped from her.

The effect of her sigh was astonishing. It conjured up all kinds of vivacity in the cave

immediately. The hum of insects at once
filled the soft atmosphere; hundreds of shadowy
butterflies began to flit about; and the child
upon the cloudlet changed his position, and
seeing Lizzette smiled, and then drew towards
her.

"I came to consult Witch Griffin," said
Lizzette in answer to the inquiry in his eyes.

"Consult me instead," the child simply
replied; and love and sympathy seemed to
beam from him. "I am Child Praim, and
older than Witch Griffin herself, though ever
a child. It is I who instruct the witch in
Nature's secrets."

And so forceful was the sympathy in the
child Praim that Lizzette's story was soon told
to him.

"And now the life of him I love is en-
dangered by a demon who haunts him. What
shall I do to help him?" she ended.

The eyes of the child grew full of dreams
again for a while, as he paused to consider;
then he replied: "With you alone, O maid,

is the cure for this distress. You, if you will,
shall change this demon into a ministering
angel."

Then he flew about among the plants and
gathered a delicate passion-flower, a heart's-
ease, and a lily from among them ; and binding
them together with a golden hair from his own
locks, gave them into Lizzette's hand, saying,
" And with these you shall do it. But," added
the child thoughtfully, "it will cost you
much, dear Maid. Are you prepared to save
him from misery at all risks and at any
cost?"

" At all risks and at any cost," returned
Lizzette in a trembling voice.

" Then take these flowers when the moon is
full into the haunted chamber, and with your
own hand place them under his pillow at
midnight," said Child Praim. " And before
you go unbind your hair, and leave behind
you for ever in this cave with me that beautiful
brooch you wear, your maiden pride, which
you have worn ever since you were a child ;

for only thus can the demon be exorcised who works your loved one ill.''

Lizzette took off her precious brooch, and, thanking Child Praim, gave it into his hand; and as she withdrew, her heart gladdened and full of gratitude, he waved farewell to her, and motioned up hundreds of fire-flies to light her through the dark, exterior cave; and these continued with her back through the gloomy forest until dawn broke.

How grateful Lizzette felt towards Child Praim is better imagined than described.

"I will obey him and do all that he said," she thought, for he is a wonderful child. And then she felt glad the witch had escaped her.

Upon Lizzette's return home the first piece of news she was told was this : "Ernest is very ill. He sent these flowers to you with a message to say so last night."

It was Lizzette's aunt who told her this.

That night the youth lay stricken with feverish weakness, as he had lain, too weak to rise, for many days. His thoughts were running on the cause of his distress, his demon visitor, and his unconfessed love for Lizzette.

He tumbled and tossed as midnight drew near, and then he quieted down into the stillness of horror; a chill expectancy stole over him. His dreaded visitor would shortly arrive to work consuming torture.

The lights began to dart around, the hot air to seethe about him. He closed his eyes to shut out, if possible, the flame-like form he knew so well: when noiselessly the door opened, and sweet Lizzette entered, her hair floating free, an atmosphere of freshness from the moonlit fields, through which she had just passed, about her.

And she was carrying in her hand the flowers Child Praim had given her.

Softly she crossed the moonlit floor, and approached her beloved in subdued agitation. Her cheek paling and flushing as she did so, her eyes full of tears and her lips trembling.

At last she reached his pillow, and gently

slipped the flowers beneath it. But, in doing
so, she bent over him; and then a spell of
overmastering love held her motionless, and a
tress of her hair fell lightly upon his face.

As he felt this sweet, cool presence near
him, instead of the burning demon, Ernest
opened his eyes in amazed delight, and, seeing
Lizzette, thought her a blissful apparition.
Yet he breathed her name, and paled with
intense joy as he gazed into her eyes. These
were so full of love and pity, however, that
the next moment he had stretched out his
arms and drawn her to his heart; and, as his
lips met hers, he found that this was indeed no
apparition, but tangible, breathing, dear Lizzette herself.

"Dearest, did my message bring you?"
he asked.

"Yes," she answered; "I came to make
you well," and her voice faltered.

"Oh! you knew, then, that I was dying for
love of you, and you had heard of the demon
who haunts me so?" he questioned eagerly.

She blushed.

"I must go," she whispered; "but come to me soon, and you shall hear all."

But he clung to her slender hands.

"Can you—will you be my wife, Lizzette?" he asked, imploringly, the question he had never dared to put before, still holding her fast.

Lizzette trembled in his arms and blushed again; her soft tears fell upon his burning cheeks.

At last he caught a sound of assent; and again their lips met in lingering kisses.

But someone was watching this interesting scene all the time. It was the nightingale; and so glad was she at the happiness she saw taking place that a volley of song escaped her quite unawares close to the window.

This startled Lizzette, so, withdrawing from her lover's embrace, she passed into the moonlit fields again, back to her own home.

It was remarkable how quickly Ernest recovered after that night. The next day he was out, and went to see Lizzette to arrange the wedding.

And it was still more remarkable how entirely the demon ghost vanished after that night.

He never appeared again. This, of course, was all owing to Child Praim's directions, and to his knowledge of Nature's secrets.

Afterwards Ernest's house was rid of that demon for ever.

It was not until the two were married, though, that Lizzette caught sight of the beautiful angel into which Child Praim had said the demon would change if she followed out his instructions, and then it was only upon rare occasions that it visited them.

At early morn it would appear, in the same chamber where the fiery demon had used to come; and the angel seemed to descend near them from the private chapel above.

It was a beautiful, bright form; but whether of man or woman, they could not tell.

It seemed like the best of both. And, with

clasped hands and hopeful mien, it would gaze
upon them and point to Heaven, as though to
say that faith, and love, and aspiration must
always be returned to the God Who gave them
their precious happiness.

Ernest and Lizzette always felt glad awe
when this angel visited them; and after it had
faded away they remembered it.

Lizzette said, "It reminds me of Child
Praim."

"It makes me think over again all the holy
thoughts I have ever treasured, and more
beside," said Ernest.

Thus, you must admit that the times when
such things as these occurred were wonderful
times, and that the present of such a house as
the one Ernest's father gave to him was indeed a remarkable present; for it grew with
his growth of its own accord, and when he
got rid of the demon there came an angel
to visit it.

WISHES AND FATE.

BROTHER and sister played together on a seashore.

The shore was like life: the sea like fate.

They dug and delved in the sand together, making a beautiful sand castle with a moat all round it. They hoped the incoming tide would presently fill the moat, and thus completed their work would be.

They dug away in the sand together diligently for a long while.

The sun's rays were like time. Then the boy paused.

In one hand his spade hung idle, while with the other he shaded his eyes from the sun to gaze over the open sea.

The tide was coming in. The waves curled and broke, scattering the spray nearer and nearer.

The boy still looked out over the sea to the horizon, where rode the gracefully-shaped sails of distant ships.

"Look at the ships, Marie," at last he cried, as the spade fell from his relaxed hold. "I wish I were a sailor. When I am a man that is what I will be. I will be a captain, and command such a ship as one of those; and I will ride the waves from one side of the world to the other."

For a moment the girl made no rejoinder; she was wrapt in her castle-making; presently, however, she too looked up and said, inquiringly, "You would be a sailor, and ride the ocean wave?"

Then she also paused, and looked out over the sea to ponder.

"Oh!" at length she exclaimed, "I should like to smooth and strengthen things all my life;" and so saying she stooped to strengthen and finish the side of the sand battlement she was making.

Just then a wave they had not watched broke nearer than the others had done, the sea water from which suddenly filled all their little moat to overflowing, and in addition to this broke upon and changed the whole aspect of the castle itself.

"Children," their mother called from the beach, "we must go home; the tide is in."

So they left their castle-building upon the shore.

Years rolled by. They grew up.

What of their wishes? The brother realised his in this way. He left his home to become a sailor. He ploughed the wondrous main from shore to shore, from continent to continent.

He grew strong in heart, and hand, and thought.

"How powerful is man, the maker of ships and compasses!" was his thought. "I, with this small instrument which man has made, find a way in the unfurrowed deep from one side of the world to the other. Glory to man's inventive powers!" he cried.

That night a storm arose. The Hand of God was in the storm, though nobody saw it.

Both ship and compasses were lost; and at midnight the sea-gulls swirled about among the troubled clouds over a pale-faced corpse.

It was the brother who had stood upon the shore as a child, and wished to ride the main on a ship of his own commanding.

He was freed from his self-sufficiency and taken to another shore, whereon to frame at heart a nobler wish in brighter sunshine.

And what of the sister—do you ask?

She grew up with a tender heart. A tender heart is easily wounded: hers was; it became filled with a longing which nearly broke it. Then the storm of life came on.

But as she lay upon the earth, pale, half dead, a swallow fell from the clouds above her. He, too, had been wounded in life's way.

Forgetting her own pain she arose to alleviate the bird's, and, tenderly taking the trembling creature in her soft hands, she bound up the broken wing.

And from that time the sister began to realise her wish. Her sympathetic touch soothed and strengthened many a sufferer.

For the Hand of God is in all the storms of life, though few see it ; and even tender hearts are sometimes broken, that new ones may be given us in their stead, and highest aspirations realised.

THE BLACKBERRY BLOSSOM.

———•◦•———

THE little white blossom grew low down by the roadside, among the grass.

"I am such a little, washed out, useless thing," she murmured to herself, at last; "would that I could be green as the leaves, red as the flowers, or black—like peoples' boots."

And her flower heart was full of discontent and longing.

It was moonlight when the blossom thus spoke, but she had been feeling what she now expressed all the bright daytime, as she had watched the passers by, especially their boots, that came so near her; and she had envied the black boots, because they got over the ground so fast and could move away!

"I am stuck here," she murmured again,

"and so tired of being nothing but a little, white blossom!"

Just then it seemed to her that a cloud had come between her and the radiant moon; but when she looked up she saw only an owl, with its soft brown feathers, and large, outspread wings, about to alight upon a branch above her.

He did so, and then, leaning his head on one side, looked at the blossom in his most melancholy wise way, as he gave vent to a dismal, crooked sort of sound, his usual note.

That must be his "How-d'-ye-do!" the blossom thought to herself, "I will speak to him."

"Good evening, Mr. Owl," she then remarked aloud; "I wonder you are not asleep; most people sleep when the dew falls."

"Ah!" said the owl, "I do the opposite; and for my part I cannot understand how any one with taste can prefer to go about in glaring sunshine; moonlight is much pleasanter. I revel in moonlight; and I like mice and beetles to eat, and damp and darkness to fly in, better than anything else you could name!"

And he leaned his head to the other side, opened his dark eyes wide, and made the same twirling sound as before, still looking fixedly at the blossom.

"That noise must mean anything and everything from an owl; he can't be saying how d'ye do now?" thought the blossom. "I will ask him another question."

"Have you gone about the world much at night, then?" was what she next said.

"Oh!" replied the owl dismally, "a very great deal, a very great deal."

"Are you then surprised to learn that I am very sad down here?" continued the blossom, too full at heart to keep silent about her trouble. "I am so tired of being nothing but a little, white blossom in the grass by the roadside," she concluded, with a sigh.

"Ah! wait, wait. What we want is worth waiting for," said the owl. And, as the blossom was wondering whether he could see into her very soul with his great, round eyes, he lifted his beautiful wings, rose again like a cloud between her and the bright moon, and vanished from sight.

The blossom's petals shook with disappointment as she watched him go.

Suddenly another voice said close to her:

" What is the matter?   Why do you sigh ?"

The blossom, in surprise, looked towards the ground whence the voice rose and saw a glow-worm ; but, never having seen one before, she at once thought it was a bit of the moon fallen from the sky above, which was speaking to her.

She looked up to the moon for the hole whence the piece had dropped; but there shone the moon above as round and perfect as usual; so she said in a fright to the bright spark, " Who are you ? "

" I am a glow-worm," returned the voice ; " and I have often seen you before, but until now you have always been asleep when I passed. What is wrong with you, that you shudder and sigh so ? "

"I am discontented," said the blossom; "so tired of being nothing but a blossom! I want to be green as the leaves, red as the flowers, or black—like people's boots. It is the want of all this which keeps me awake and makes me shudder and sigh," she concluded.

"Poor thing!" exclaimed the glow-worm; "I am sorry for you, and my advice is just keep up your spirits, for whatever we want in this world never comes the faster through our getting low-spirited about it."

"But do you think I ever shall be what I want to be?" persisted the blossom, so thankful at last to put the question, which had burned within her for so long. "Do you think there is any chance of it?"

"To tell the truth," the glow-worm answered, "it would not surprise me, if you were in the end to become *just* what you wanted to be in the beginning."

The blossom at this rejoinder again shook all over, but now it was with pleasure.

"You see," the glow-worm continued,

"nothing could be stranger or more wonderful than my own experience, for instance.
I began life a most ordinary creature, a sort
of beetle, but ugly in colour as a slug.
Instead of lamenting my ugliness, however,
I determined to make the best of it; I tried
my hardest to be cheerful and attract my
fellows in spite of it; and now they tell me
I shine like the beautiful moon herself as I
go by. Wonderful! isn't it," she again exclaimed, "that I, the ugly slug, should in
any way resemble the beautiful moon? In
my opinion, therefore, you need not despair,
for there is never any telling what you may
become in this world if only you keep up your
spirits and do your duty."

And, wishing the blossom good night, the
glow worm moved away.

How gladly the blossom gazed after it, now
that her anxiety had been appeased; the very
dew seemed to heal her sorrow, and she slept.

The next morning bright was she directly
she awoke, as happy as possible, for the owl's

words rang in her mind, "What we want is worth waiting for," and the glow-worm's "Be cheerful."

"I will wait and be cheerful," she said to herself, "and perhaps even I shall be some day as green as the leaves, as red as the flowers, and as black as people's boots."

"Hullo!" exclaimed some one, and at the same time the little blossom felt herself sprung upon, and almost covered by something.

"Oh, dear!" she called out. "Who is this?"

"I beg your pardon!" said the same voice, and the next instant the blossom was free again, for the thing, whatever it was, had gone as suddenly as it had come.

Then, upon a neighbouring blade of grass, she saw the intruder alight—a grasshopper.

"You took me quite by surprise!" observed the blossom to him, rather testily. "I wish another time you wouldn't jump all over one's face in that manner: it's so unpleasant!"

"Dear, dear, how unlucky I am!" replied the

grasshopper, in an apologetic manner. " The last time I had a good jump I annoyed a hare-bell. Dear Madam! do forgive me! It is so difficult to calculate where I shall be after one of my flying leaps. If you only knew," he continued, "how difficult it is to aim straight with your own body when you jump from twenty to thirty times its length, I believe you would forgive me," he ended.

" If you can't tell where you will be when you have jumped, why don't you stand still?" continued the blossom, still ruffled.

" I sometimes do ; I am doing so now, you see," returned the talkative grasshopper ; " but I can't stand still always. I can take short jumps, too, sometimes ; but then, sooner or later, a fellow must see something of the world ; and, when I feel this come over me, I just take one of my flying leaps, and then, you see, though I don't know exactly where I shall be at the end of it, at least I know that I shall get a change and see something fresh."

And before the blossom could make further

rejoinder, the grasshopper had quite disappeared.

"Oh!" she thought to herself, "what a good thing it is I can't jump about in that way when I feel discontented; I should be flying into somebody's face, as sure as anything, if I did."

And now she was vexed with herself for having been vexed with the jumping grasshopper, who meant no harm.

That night, when the sun had set and the stars were shining, a strange thing befell the the little blackberry blossom.

One by one her petals began to fall from her to the ground, and not through shuddering and sighing, for now she was calm and happy.

The owl saw it with his great, round eyes, for he had come to pay her another call; and the stars might have seen it had they not been twinkling too busily to see at all; but the little blossom herself felt more astonished than any one else could have felt at what was happening to her.

She waited silently, wondering what could fall from her next; and you may fancy her joy when morning revealed that she was no longer a little, white blossom, but a small, lumpy berry, *as green as the leaves*.

Strangely contented now felt the little thing, and, as she grew in the grass by the roadside, day by day and night after night, you could not have found a happier creature anywhere than was she.

"There is no telling what may happen next," was what she began to think to herself at this time, "in a world where wonderful changes come about every day."

And the owl quite agreed with her, and would have given her a great deal more of his good advice, but when he came to see her now she was always contentedly asleep.

And, fancy the berry's amazement when, a week or two later, another change befell her!

She turned red—red as the flowers, as the bright corn-poppies are!

"Oh!" she exclaimed, joyfully; "nothing is too good to be true in this wonderful world! Here am I as red as the flowers now—turned from green to red! If only I could end my days by being as black as people's boots I should die happy."

"You won't need to die at all, I daresay," said a voice, which she remembered to have heard before, close beside her. "You will most likely be eaten up, and that will save you the trouble of dying, anyhow."

And the berry again saw her acquaintance, the grasshopper, who had turned up suddenly.

"What do you mean by being eaten up?" she asked, rather timidly.

"Just what I say, dear Madam," replied the grasshopper, quickly. "Since I last had the misfortune to jump upon you as a little, white blossom, I have jumped about the world a very great deal, and learnt much. Among other things, I now know that, since you have changed into a berry, if you turn black you run the risk of being eaten up."

"But what do you mean by that?" again the berry asked.

"Ah! well, my dear Madam, I see I must explain myself," the grasshopper went on. "To be eaten up is to be put out of this existence into somebody else's, quite involuntarily. Many people come to an end by being eaten up, and many others come to an end by dying, and, as to which you prefer, why, it's all a matter of taste! I personally prefer the thought of dying; but only the other day I was talking with a friend of mine, a mushroom, and if she didn't tell me she positively looked forward to being eaten up! She said she quite looked forward to being taken from the fields some day in a can, and swallowed by a biped!"

"And what, pray, is a biped!" asked the berry in agitation.

"Oh!" returned the grasshopper, "a biped is a huge animal they call man. He has only two legs to go upon, no wings at all, and he is a very poor jumper; yet he seems to get a

good deal of his own way in the world, in spite
of his disadvantages. I myself always keep
out of his way, for he is desperately clumsy,
and breaks down the tallest blades of grass
cruelly wherever he treads."

" Dear !" exclaimed the berry, again amazed.
" Do you say that the mushroom *looks forward*
to being eaten up by a biped ? "

" Well, as I said before, you know," continued the grasshopper, "there is no ac-
counting for tastes, and I could scarcely make
out what she meant, though she tried to explain it ; but she did positively assure me that
the thought of being eaten up, or fulfilling her
destiny, or whatever it was, made her thrill
with pleasure. But it's my opinion," concluded the grass-hopper, lowering his voice
confidentially, "that as she does not know
what it is to thrill at all, she just passes the
time by feeling pleasantly morbid about being
eaten up instead."

And away he went in his usual hurry, while
the berry was left to think over his words.

She rather began to fear this "being eaten up." But in the end she made up her mind that, if she had become all that she wanted to be—green as the leaves, red as the flowers, and black like people's boots before long, she would be—yes, even if eaten up, she thought —satisfied.

And when, a short time afterwards, the golden sunshine of an autumn afternoon actually turned the red berry into a fine, large, ripe blackberry, blacker far than the cleanest, best polished pair of boots, she was so thoroughly happy and contented, and grateful and glad, that if the largest small boy biped had come by on his way to school and eaten her up whole, just as she was, she would not have minded in the very least, because she had now become all that she had ever wanted to be!

She had left her blossom time far behind, and changed into beautiful, ripe fruit.

LOVE AND THE SPRING-TIME.

———•◦•———

IT was spring-time. The goddess of Love was awaking just as the West wind blew by; and she waved to him such love-power as made the West wind sigh again.

"Go, breathe, and blow over the flowers with the burden of love I give thee. Woo them, till each flower-heart shall yield to love, and teach thee a priceless truth! Let thy breathing and blowing this spring-time be all of love! And before those flowers that heed thee not, as the boundless wind shalt thou appear in the form of an ethereal cupid, while obeying this my decree."

So away flew the West wind, highly delighted with his commission. He had often thought how delightful it would be to be able to assume a form occasionally: and then, to have orders from the goddess of Love herself to make love to all the flowers— nothing so much to his taste as this had ever happened to him before!

The first flower he came across was the snowdrop. She stood, her dainty head hanging petulant and free, on a patch of earth from which the snow had lately been melted.

New warmth had stolen into the sun's rays from between the fitful clouds, and driven the snow from the earth's frozen bosom; thus the white snowdrop was clearly distinguishable against the dark soil.

At once the West wind blew round and about her, breathing of tenderness; but the snowdrop would have nothing to do with him. She turned her head away and nodded in exactly the opposite direction; and the more amorously the West wind blew the more emphatically the snowdrop nodded her dainty head in just the opposite direction, as though to declare that she would not submit to his caresses.

The West wind was repulsed, and began to fume in his sighing. But a robin, who, with bright eye and warm breast, stood near where the incident occurred, twittered out—

" It is of no use your coming to woo our little snowdrop. She plighted her troth to the North wind long ago, directly she came up; and I have often heard her say she would be true to him. And to be true to the one lover, the snowdrop says you must be cold to the other."

" Oh, I see—I see ! " said the rejected West wind, ill-pleased for all that; he wanted to kiss the dainty snowdrop so much.

And immediately he blew elsewhere, not forgetting his disappointment, however, until the golden crocuses were all a-bloom, and had received him with open hearts, whispering—

" Full love maketh full joy ! "

Meanwhile the primroses had crept, chilled, into existence. They were looking almost too

pale and timid to be seen; but when they met
the West wind and his balmy breathing over
the lea, they grew finer and bloomed gra-
ciously, yielding to him in return a balmy fragrance. And, when approached by the West
wind with his burden of love, they whispered,
" In the delicacy of love is ineffable sweetness ! "

And the West wind hovered and still
breathed over the primroses, while they
bloomed into greater beauty and more delicate fragrance.

Then, at the dawn of day, on went the wind
to a hillside where he found the first Lent lily
blooming alone; tall, green blades were her
only companions. She stood, coy and *difficile*,
in the half-light of the mysterious dawn, as he
came up. He blew tenderly near the gentle
flower, but she heeded him not; so then he
appeared in the form of a shadowy cupid, and
bowed low to the ground before her. Now, to
his joy, she noticed him. A slight tremor
betrayed this, and when he approached and

laid his burden of love over her, she swayed as only so slender a stem could sway beneath it, and yielding him a fragile kiss, sighed out—"Love's lightest touch is full of magic power!"

And the West wind sighed too, for he was feeling it.

But, as the sun rose, the Lent lily withdrew into herself, and the shadowy form of Cupid merged into the boundless West wind again, hurrying on with his errand.

How different were the daffodowndillies when he reached the gardens where they grew!

In groups they stood, bathed in light, and at once they received the wind, as gladly as they did the joyous sunshine.

"There is love for the having of all," said they; "only the too particular need starve for want of it."

And their heavy, golden heads moved and met the West wind's amorous blowing as readily as did the tree-branches.

But the wind was learning all this time how different was the quality of the love he awoke in the different flowers.

When he drew near the hyacinths, that rose luxuriously from garden-beds freshly sprinkled with April showers, their sweetness gradually overpowered him, and, for a moment, he, as the shadowy Cupid, lay fainting at the foot of a regal, white hyacinth, the embodiment of fragrance.

"Ah! learn," said the queenly flower, as he recovered himself, "that love too rashly probed may be more powerful than you yourself are.   Beware how you rouse love!"

And the burden the West wind carried grew heavier than ever, for perfume and love from the regal white hyacinth slid into it, and the wind blew on, charged with an ominous truth.

Joy from the meadows now met him.

The hawthorn was a-bloom in the hedges, the cowslips, and the buttercups and daisies in the fields.

"It is the spring of the year; May is here!

and Love is the spring of life!'' sang the haw-thorn, under the West wind's caress.

And the daisies, when he came up to them, whispered, "You find even us out! True love ever valued modesty!''

Then the buttercups yielded him golden kisses, saying, "Priceless are love's pure greetings!''

And the cowslips whispered with myriad responses to his breathing, "Love lavishes gifts—lavishes gifts!''

Still onward the West wind bounded, and now he came to convent grounds.

Lilac and laburnum trees shaded the paths there. The wind revelled among them.

The delicately-poised laburnum flowers swayed at once to his gentle touch, murmuring, "Mutual love maketh one life.''

And though at first the lilac seemed stiff as the West wind drew near, she in the end yielded such a volley of delicious perfume as clearly proved that "a stiff form may shield a heart redolent with love.''

K

Sweet nuns walked in these paths and along the terraces. In their devout faces rested holy thought: but the West wind only bathed them the more with the god-given burden he carried.

The pensive maids glowed and shuddered, and strove with the fond dreams of earthly love which began to beset their hearts.

The West wind grieved as they resisted, for he thought them the fairest of all earth's flowers, and the lessons that love from their hearts would have taught him he longed to know; but, since they would not yield to him, on he blew till he found sweet violets blowing in a cloister corner. They were well-nigh hidden from sight; but he found them out, and pausing gently above, laid his burden of love low down, till at last it reached the flowers themselves, concealed under the green leaves.

The response the violets then gave was so searchingly sweet that the West wind trembled and shook; their sweetness was almost more than he could bear; and, as he trembled entranced by their ineffable fragrance, he heard them whisper, "Purest, sweetest love is found in lowliest hearts."

And for long moments the West wind hung over the sweet, *sweet* violets.

But time was meanwhile wearing on.

And the wind knew from the bearing of the rosebuds that summer was close at hand, and the time of his spring wooing near an end. So driving away from the convent grounds, he hastened that he might reach the river where he knew forget-me-nots grew, before his wooing-time should be over.

As he approached the bank he could see that some of the forget-me-nots were out, and he rushed among the tall iris leaves to greet them, and for the last time to assume the form of a cupid. Bending towards the flowers, he showered kisses upon their tranquil blue eyes until they trembled and sighed in their meditation. "Here is love, love!" they exclaimed.

And just as summer came up, to change

the West wind into the South wind and end
his wooing time altogether, the shadowy form
of Cupid stood with his arms enfolding the
dear forget-me-nots who were yielding him
kisses, murmuring, " Ah ! then for love's dear
sake forget us not, for of all the treasures
memory holds, those love has sanctified are
the most precious."

And then summer came on ; and never
again could the boundless West wind assume
a form. But the lessons of love which the
flowers had taught him he never forgot. And
every spring-time as he breathes, and blows,
and bounds over hill and dale, and garden and
field, he is rife with love presage and heavy
with ruth.

WERTHEIMER, LEA & CO., PRINTERS, CIRCUS PLACE, LONDON WALL, E.C.